# Big Bird and Little Bird's

CTW
SESAME STREET

# BIG & LITTLE BOOK

### BY EMILY PERL KINGSLEY • Illustrated by A. DELANEY

*Featuring Jim Henson's Sesame Street Muppets*

"I like big things!"
Big Bird said.

"I like little things!"
Little Bird said.

## A SESAME STREET / A GOLDEN BOOK

Published by Western Publishing Company, Inc. in cooperation with Children's Television Workshop. © 1983, 1977
Children's Television Workshop. Muppet characters © 1983, 1977 Muppets, Inc. All rights reserved. Printed in the U.S.A.
No part of this book may be reproduced or copied in any form without written permission from the publisher.
Big Bird and Little Bird are trademarks of Muppets, Inc. Sesame Street® and the Sesame Street sign are trademarks and service marks
of Children's Television Workshop. GOLDEN®, GOLDEN® & DESIGN, A GOLDEN SHAPE BOOK®, and A GOLDEN BOOK® are trademarks
of Western Publishing Company, Inc. ISBN 0-307-58011-3 ISBN 0-307-68989-1 (lib. bdg.)    D E F G H I J

"I like big balloons."

"I like little things best,"
said Little Bird, "but there's one
big thing I really like."

"You!"

"I like little balloons."

"I like molehills."

"I like goldfish."

"I like ships."

"I like rowboats."

"I like to play the tuba."

"I like to play the piccolo."

"I like freight trains."

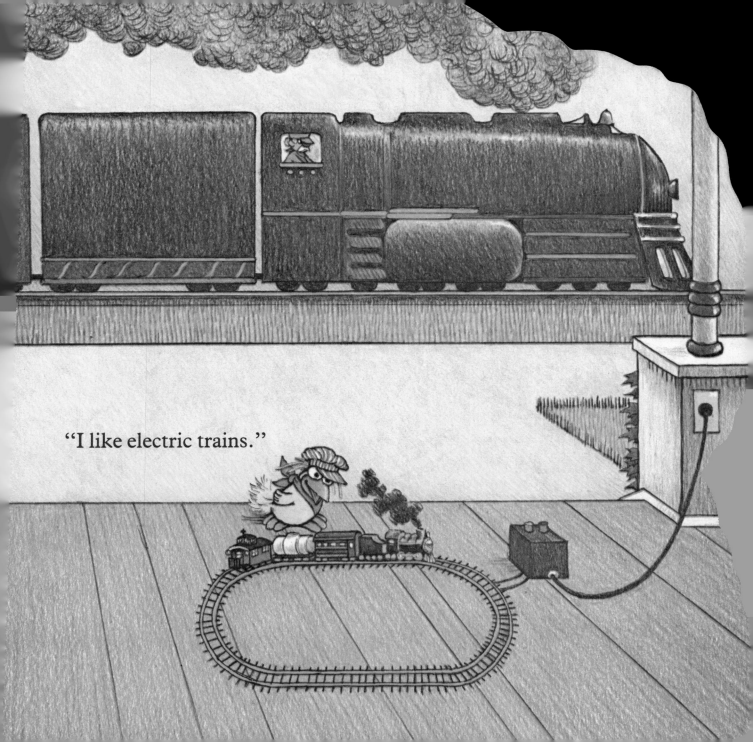

"I like electric trains."

"I like Great Danes."

"I like Chihuahuas."

"I like elephants."

"I like watermelons."

"I like grapes."

"I like big things best,"
said Big Bird, "but there's one
little thing I like a lot."